For Carol

Peter May was born and raised in Scotland. He was an award-winning journalist at the age of twenty-one and a published novelist at twenty-six. When his first book was adapted as a major drama series for the BBC, he quit journalism and during the high-octane fifteen years that followed, became one of Scotland's most successful television dramatists. He created three prime-time drama series, presided over two of the highest-rated serials in his homeland as script editor and producer, and worked on more than 1,000 episodes of ratings-topping drama before deciding to leave television to return to his first love, writing novels.

His passion for detailed research for his books has taken him behind the closed doors of the Chinese Police force, to the kitchen of a three-star Michelin chef, and down the Paris catacombs; he has worked as an online private detective, was inducted as a Chevalier of the Grand Order of Gaillac wines and earned honorary membership of the Chinese Crime Writers' Association.

He has won several literature awards in France and received the USA's Barry Award for *The Blackhouse*, the first in his internationally bestselling Lewis Trilogy, and the ITV Crime Thriller Awards Book Club Best Read for *Entry Island*.

He now lives in south-west France with his wife, writer Janice Hally.

BY PETER MAY

The Enzo Files

Extraordinary People
The Critic
Blacklight Blue
Freeze Frame
Blowback

The China Thrillers

The Firemaker
The Fourth Sacrifice
The Killing Room
Snakehead
The Runner
Chinese Whispers

The Lewis Trilogy

The Blackhouse
The Lewis Man
The Chessmen

Standalone Novels

Entry Island
Runaway
Coffin Road

Non-fiction

Hebrides with David Wilson

PETER MAY

THE
FOURTH
SACRIFICE

riverrun

First published in Great Britain in 2000 by Coronet Books
This paperback edition published in 2016 by

riverrun
an imprint of
Quercus Editions Ltd
Carmelite House
50 Victoria Embankment
London EC4Y 0DZ

An Hachette UK company

A CIP catalogue record for this book is available
from the British Library

ISBN 978 1 78429 269 0
EBOOK ISBN 978 1 78087 957 4

10 9 8 7 6 5 4 3 2

Typeset by CC Book Production

Printed and bound in Great Britain by Clays Ltd, St Ives plc

PROLOGUE

By now he knows he is going to die. And he feels something like relief. No more long, lonely nights and tortured dreams. He can release all those dark feelings that he has carried through life like some great weight strapped to his back, causing him to stoop and stagger and bend at the knees. Still this knowledge, that death is close enough almost to touch, is not without fear. But the fear has retreated with the effects of the drug, and lurks somewhere just beyond consciousness.

He is only vaguely aware of those things around him that have been so familiar these last months: the scarred and naked walls, the rusted window frames, the washing hanging out to dry in the glassed-in balcony beyond the screen door. There is still a smell of stale cooking in the air, and sometimes the occasional hint of raw sewage that rises from the drains in the street four floors below, especially when it rains, like now. He hears the rain pattering on the windowpanes, blurring the lights of the apartment block opposite, like the tears that he can feel, warm and salty, on his cheeks. Only now does he succumb to an overwhelming sense of sadness. What futility! His life, the lives of his parents, and of their parents before them. What did any of them mean? What point had there been?

Now he feels rough hands forcing him to his knees, and a cord is passed over his head, a flash of red characters on white card as it drops to hang around his neck. Now his hands are drawn behind his back, and he feels the soft, familiar texture of silk as it tightens around his wrists, grazing and bruising. He would have been gentler with it. Despite the best efforts of the drug, his fear is re-emerging now, rising in his throat like bile. He sees a flash of light on dark, dull metal and a hand pushes his head forward and down. No point in resistance. No point in anything, not even regret. And yet it is there, big and scary and casting a shadow in his consciousness, fighting for space alongside his fear.

He is aware of the figure on his right, and he sees the shadow of the rising blade trace its pattern across the pale linoleum. He swallows and wonders if he will feel any pain. How good is his executioner? And then, fleetingly, he wonders if the brain ceases the instant the head is severed. He hears the swish of the blade and has a sharp intake of breath.

No, there is no pain, he realises, as for a moment, before blackness, the room spins crazily and he sees the twin jets of blood spewing from the strange apparition of his own headless body as it topples forward. But he will never be able to tell anyone. So many things he will never be able to tell.

CHAPTER ONE

I

The rain fell like tears from a leaden Beijing sky. Ironic, Margaret thought, for hers had long since dried up. From the shelter of her balcony on the sixth floor she could see, across the treetops in the park opposite, the dull reflection of a tiny pavilion in the rain-spotted lake. Above the rumble of traffic, and the mournful banter of furriers in the street below, she could hear the wail of a single-stringed violin and the sad cadences of a woman's voice breathing passion into a song from the Peking Opera.

Margaret moved back into her hotel room and slipped a light coat over her blouse and jeans. She had told herself she had chosen this hotel because of its proximity to the American Embassy. It was nothing to do with the park across the road. That's what she had told herself. But Ritan Park was her last connection to him. A place where the death of a man had first brought them together and, in the end, forced them apart. Just one more failure in a life that seemed destined always to let her down. She lifted her umbrella and closed the door firmly behind her, resolved finally to act on a decision she had delayed for too long.

On the fourth floor, an elderly woman with brassy lacquered hair and too much make-up stepped on to the elevator. Margaret saw that she was wearing a name badge on the lapel of her blue suit jacket. Dot McKinlay, it read. Margaret registered some surprise. Mostly the Ritan Hotel was filled with the wealthy but unsophisticated wives of Russian traders, desperate to spend their roubles before the exchange rate fell any further. The woman drew painted lips back across long, slightly yellowed teeth in what she clearly imagined was a smile.

'Where y'awl from?' she drawled.

Margaret's heart sank. 'The sixth floor,' she said, keeping her eyes firmly fixed on the illuminated numbers above the door, willing them to descend more quickly.

But Dot just laughed, heartily, as if she had enjoyed the joke. 'Ah do like a sense of humour,' she said. 'Y'awl from the north, that's for sure. We're from the south. Louisiana. Only thing further south than us is the Gulf of Mexico.' She laughed again, as if demonstrating that southerners could be just as amusing as northerners. 'Ol' Dot's Travellin' Grannies, that's what they call us. We been all over. Just our luck to choose China during the rice crisis. Don't you just get sick of those noodles?' She leaned in confidentially. 'And if Ah'd known this hotel was gonna be so full of goddamn Ruskies, Ah'd 'a booked us in somewheres else.' She nodded emphatically. 'But it's great to know there's a fellow American on board. Even if ya do come from the sixth floor.' She grinned. 'Why don't y'awl join us for a drink tonight?'

Margaret glanced at her. 'I'm afraid that won't be possible,' she said. 'I'm leaving tomorrow.'

The doors opened on the ground floor as Dot was about to express her disappointment, and Margaret hurried away past a group of a dozen or so elderly ladies all sporting name badges. She heard Dot greeting them with, 'Hey, you'll never guess who that was . . .'

No, Margaret thought as she pushed through glass doors and out into the sticky, warm rain, they never would. Not in a million years. The two security men at the gate glowered at her as she opened her umbrella on the way out. It was only in the last couple of weeks that Western newsmen had stopped hanging about the gate in the hope of getting photographs or an interview. The security guards in their brown uniforms, privately hired by the hotel, had been forced to take their duties seriously, instead of sitting around all day smoking and looking important. They didn't much like Margaret.

She ran the gauntlet of some half-hearted stall owners who thought she might be Russian and interested in the furs that hung row upon row under dripping canopies. But most of them knew her by now and didn't give her a second glance, sitting folded up on tiny stools, nursing jars of cold green tea, smoking acrid-smelling cigarettes and spitting noisily on the sidewalk. Everywhere you looked here, the names of shops and restaurants were written in the distinctive Cyrillic Russian alphabet. You could almost believe you were in some seedy corner of Moscow, if it wasn't for the Chinese faces. Someone had lit a brazier, in preparation for an early lunch, and smoke mingled with the mist and rain. Margaret almost stepped into the path of several bicycles, alerted only at the last moment by a flurry of bells. Oriental faces glared at her from glistening hooded capes. She grasped the railing at the edge of the pavement and held tightly, overcome by a moment of giddiness. She breathed deeply and steadied herself. She had not realised until now just how stressful this was going to be.

To delay the moment, she took the route through the park, although she would have denied, if asked, that she was procrastinating. But she knew immediately it was a mistake. The place was too full of memories and regrets. She hurried past small damp groups of people practising *tai ch'i* under the trees, and out through the south gate. Again she took a circuitous route, along Guanghua Road and down Silk Street, past the new visa block in the Bruce Compound of the American Embassy. Women in white masks and blue smocks swept wet leaves from the gutters with old-fashioned brooms. Dismal marketeers sat under the shelter of trees opposite their empty stalls, tourists kept away by the rain.

A young woman with cropped hair approached Margaret hopefully. 'CD lom?' she said. 'CD music? Looka, looka, I have new ones.'

Margaret shook her head and hurried by. A very thin young man in a dark suit and white shirt with no tie approached. 'Shanja dollah?'

'No!' Margaret snapped at him, and stepped briskly away